W9-ASD-235

By Julie Andrews Edwards
and Emma Walton Hamilton

SIMEON'S GIFT

Illustrated by Gennady Spirin

HarperCollins*Publishers*

Simeon's Gift

Text copyright © 2003 by Wellspring LLC
Illustrations copyright © 2003 by Gennady Spirin
Printed in the United States of America. All rights reserved.
www.harperchildrens.com

Library of Congress Cataloging-in-Publication Data
Edwards, Julie, date.
    Simeon's gift / by Julie Andrews and Emma Walton Hamilton ; illustrated by
Gennady Spirin.
       p.   cm. — (The Julie Andrews collection)
    Summary: A humble musician sets out to find his muse and is overwhelmed by all he sees,
until he discovers within himself his true gift.
    ISBN 0-06-008914-8 — ISBN 0-06-008915-6 (lib. bdg.)
    [1. Musicians—Fiction. 2. Self-realization—Fiction.]   I. Hamilton, Emma Walton.
II. Spirin, Gennady, ill. III. Title. IV. Series.
PZ7.E2562 Si   2003   2002003538
[E]—dc21   CIP
                                                   AC

Typography by Jeanne L. Hogle
2 3 4 5 6 7 8 9 10
❖

For our fathers
—J.A.E. and F.W.H.

For my love's sons:
Ilya, Gennady, Andrei
—G.S.

long time ago, when castles and monasteries dotted the land and knights went forth to do brave deeds, when women wove beautiful tapestries and minstrels played for pauper and prince alike, there lived a humble musician named Simeon. Though uneducated and penniless, he was a gentle, nature-loving man, and music was his passion.

He spent his days playing his lute and singing songs of the countryside for the entertainment of his fellow villagers. He loved a beautiful lady of noble birth named Sorrel, and she loved him, yet he felt ashamed and unworthy of her love. He longed to offer her all the comforts of life, but his lowly status and the simplicity of his art could provide no more than a meager existence.

Simeon concluded that the only way to
better himself was to experience the world beyond
his. If he could hear new sounds—new rhythms, new
voices—he might be able to free the music he was certain lay
deep in his soul. Perhaps then he could move beyond singing the
songs of others. . . .

Perhaps then he could *create* songs that others would sing.

With a heavy heart, he bade farewell to his beloved Sorrel,
promising to return with gifts worthy of her faith and patience. He set
out, carrying his precious lute, traveling many days, many miles.
Often he felt lonely and homesick, but he took comfort from the
sounds of the birds and the animals, the whispering trees, and
the river nearby, and when the need for sleep overcame
him, he rested under the stars.

One morning, he was awakened by the distant sound of drums. Curious to find the source, he hastened in their direction, his stride matching their insistent beat. He came upon an encampment of soldiers practicing their drills and disciplines. The soldiers welcomed him, and he spent several days in their company, listening to the powerful drums and noticing the ways in which they invigorated his spirit. He embraced the new rhythms—but though they energized his songs, he knew there was still more to learn. When the soldiers went their way, Simeon went his.

He returned to the river
and found himself on the same path as a
kindly monk, who invited him to join his brothers
for supper at the abbey. Grateful for their hospitality,
Simeon knelt with them in evening prayer, and when their
voices raised in worship, his spirits soared. Their harmonic
chanting transported him, and for a moment he felt at one with all
creation. In the days that followed, he tried adding those harmonies to
his songs, but though they brought new color to his melodies, still he felt
the need to journey on.

Finding the river once again, he saw a great walled city in the
distance, its spires and turrets shimmering and twinkling in the
morning light. Simeon hesitated, knowing that in the opposite
direction lay home and his devoted Sorrel. His heart ached
to see her again, but the melodic murmur of the river
reminded him that the task he had set himself was
far from complete. With a sigh, he moved
on towards the city.

The road was busy with laborers, merchants, farmers, and fishermen, streaming into the city and out of it. Simeon fell into step beside a young poet, and as they walked and talked, he marveled at his companion's use of language and how it evoked such powerful images and feelings. He reflected on the words to his own simple songs, but though they now held a new importance, he became more and more aware of his thirst for knowledge.

The city was a cacophony!

Hooves clattered on the cobblestones, carts rattled as they passed, voices chattered in doorways and windows. The bells from the cathedral rang sonorously, and as he opened the towering doors, resonant chords from the great organ within seemed to shake the ground beneath him. Trumpets heralding the arrival of the archbishop rang in the air.

For days, Simeon wandered about the city. Music seemed to be *everywhere*. He heard and saw instruments unlike any he had ever known . . . harps, fiddles, all manner of flutes and pipes. And each one beckoned to him. Eager to learn from them all, he absorbed everything he could, trying this, embracing that, but the rhythms, the harmonies, the words, the vibrations began to hammer at his senses until they became indistinguishable from one another. The more he took in, the more confused he became.

Overwhelmed and unable to make sense of the discord in his head, he despaired. He felt that he had learned nothing . . . that he *knew* nothing. Compared to all that he had seen and the great music and poetry he had heard, his own attempts at song seemed small and insignificant. Weary of spirit, he believed that even the music he loved had deserted him.

"I have lost my way," he reflected sadly. "I have nothing to offer. All I have left is my lute, and that is of no use to me now."

Empty-handed and without even the gifts he had promised, he was suddenly overwhelmed with the desire to see his beloved Sorrel and to hold her in his arms once again.

The swiftest way home was to ride the river. With resolve, he traded his precious lute for an old canoe, some vegetables and fruit, and a handful of grains. He fashioned a mast from a stout piece of wood, and using his shirt as a sail and the red cloth that had carried his provisions as a canopy, he set off downstream.

Without his lute and his music, it was a long and lonely voyage.

One afternoon, as he was preparing a humble meal for himself, a brightly colored bird flew onto the mast of his canoe. The bird cocked its head and eyed his supper hungrily.

"I don't have much to offer," Simeon called to him, "but I have little appetite, and you're welcome to what there is." He scattered the handful of grains, and the bird flew down and ate every last one.

To Simeon's surprise, as he continued on his journey, the little bird followed him. Each day he expected it to fly away, but each day it stayed by his side. He was grateful for its company and soothed by the sweet song it sang. The confusion in his head began to subside.

Days passed, and one morning, Simeon noticed a different tone in the bird's song . . . a warning. He saw some men fishing on the riverbank. They had just captured a glorious pink-and-golden fish—the most beautiful Simeon had ever seen. His heart sank at the thought of its fate.

"Gentlemen," he called, as he came abreast of them, "I have here some fine vegetables and fruit. I would be willing to trade them all in return for that one beautiful fish."

The men were delighted. Fish were plentiful enough, but fresh fruit and vegetables were hard to come by. So the exchange was made.

Simeon sailed on and gently released the shimmering creature back into the water where it belonged. It swam in delighted circles for a moment, and the bird chirruped happily above. Then, miraculously, like the bird, the fish stayed close and followed the canoe on its journey.

With two companions to cheer him, Simeon felt much happier. He listened to the bird singing gaily on the mast and the golden fish splashing and dancing in the river, and little by little their music revived his weary soul.

Enchanted by their sounds, he cut a sturdy reed from the riverbank and began to fashion a flute. As he carved and whittled each day, an intriguing melody stirred in his head. Each evening, nightingales, crickets, owls, and bullfrogs inspired harmonies that wove through his mind like the strands of mist that creep across the river before dawn.

One morning, a beautiful fawn emerged through the trees. She tiptoed to the water's edge, limping as though in pain. When Simeon approached her, she shied away, but the bird called out to her in a trilling voice. After a moment, she nervously returned and allowed Simeon to examine her tiny hoof.

Speaking to her in gentle tones, he pried out an offending pebble, all the while telling of his journey, his newfound friends, and how his desire to see his beloved Sorrel had grown stronger with each passing day.

With renewed urgency, he pushed away from the shore and trimmed the sail of his canoe. To his delight and amazement, the little fawn kept pace with him along the river path—the clip-clopping of her dainty hooves offering a rhythm to the new theme echoing in his head.

And so the bird, the fish, the fawn, and the
man with the flute in the canoe with the sail and
the bright-red sunshade journeyed on together . . .
and after several days they came within sight of his village.

Word of Simeon's arrival spread quickly. Sorrel came running
towards him, and then at last she was in his arms. There was a time
of hugging and kissing, of telling and laughing and crying.

Finally, Simeon introduced his three companions.

"Oh, dear Simeon!" cried Sorrel. "What wonderful gifts you bring!
A bird to sing to us, a fish to swim in our river, and a beautiful fawn,
who will stay by my side and lay her head in my lap when I am
daydreaming. But *most* wonderful of all, beloved, is that you
are home, and we are together once again."

In his joy, Simeon suddenly heard the entire song in his head and in his heart. He picked up his flute, and all the music that had been building within him for so long poured forth in one complete and perfect melody. When it was finished, the look of rapture on Sorrel's face told him that all the gifts in the world could not have honored her more.

As the years passed, Simeon's one song led to many more, and his talent became revered across the land. Throughout his life—and he lived a very long life indeed—Simeon never forgot the lesson he had learned as a humble musician: that a true and brave heart can find a way, if it will only trust in all the wonders under God's canopy.